Catch Me If You Can

Tia Marlee

A Novel Choice Press

Contents

To my wonderful beta readers, Gari, Heather, Valarie, Jane and Jannell. You help keep me on track, and I wouldn't be the author I am without your support.

One

CAROLINE

THE FLASHING BLUE AND red lights in my rearview mirror make my stomach drop. Not again. This is the third time this month, and I already know exactly who's going to saunter up to my window with that infuriating smirk on his face.

I pull my sedan to the side of the road and take a deep breath. Five years of practicing law in Boston, handling cutthroat divorces where millions were at stake, and somehow Officer Ben Ramirez of the Firelight Falls Police Department gets under my skin more than any opposing counsel ever could.

I roll down my window as he approaches, his broad shoulders filling out that crisp uniform in a way that should be illegal. The summer sun glints off his badge, and despite my annoyance, I notice the way his dark eyes crinkle at the corners when he spots me.

"Ms. Colton," he says, pulling off his sunglasses with theatrical slowness. "We've got to stop meeting like this."

"Officer Ramirez." I grip the steering wheel tighter. "Let me guess. I was going five miles over the speed limit on a completely empty road?"

He leans down, resting his forearms on my window frame, bringing with him the scent of pine and something uniquely *him*. "Seven, actually. But who's counting?"

I am. I'm counting every single interaction I've had with this man since I moved back to Firelight Falls to help my mother after I found out she was sick. What was supposed to be a temporary arrangement has stretched into more, and somehow I've managed to cross paths with the town's most beloved officer at every turn.

"Don't you have actual criminals to chase?" I ask, digging through my purse for my license and registration before he can ask.

"In Firelight Falls?" He laughs, and the sound does something weird to my chest that I refuse to acknowledge. "The most criminal activity we've had this month was when Mrs. Henderson's chicken escaped and terrorized the patrons at the Texan Café."

I hand over my documents. "Sounds thrilling."

"You have no idea." He studies my license, though I know he doesn't need to. "You know, most people who move back to small towns are looking to slow down, not speed up."

"I'm not most people."

"That," he says, handing back my license with a look that's far too perceptive, "is becoming increasingly clear, Counselor."

The way he says my professional title sounds vaguely like an insult, but there's a warmth in his voice that confuses me. I've built my career on reading people, on finding the cracks in their stories during depositions, but Ben Ramirez is frustratingly difficult to categorize.

"Are you going to write me a ticket, Officer, or are we just going to chat about my driving habits all afternoon?"

He straightens up, tapping my license against his palm. "Consider this a friendly warning. Next time, I can't let it slide."

"How generous."

"I'm known for my generosity." His smile widens. "Welcome home, Caroline. Again."

He walks back to his cruiser, and I absolutely do not watch him go in my rearview mirror. I definitely don't notice the way his uniform pants fit perfectly or how confident his stride is.

I put the car in drive and pull back onto the road, this time precisely at the speed limit. As I drive toward my brother's house, I remind myself he's just a guy. My brother's friend, even. No one important.

Officer Ben Ramirez and his infuriating smile are just scenery.

The problem with scenery is you're not supposed to notice it three times a month.

Two

BEN

I WATCH CAROLINE COLTON's silver sedan drive away, exactly at the speed limit this time. She's stubborn, I'll give her that.

I slide back into my cruiser and set my sunglasses on the dashboard. Three times I've pulled her over, and three times she's looked at me like I'm the bane of her existence—which is a shame, because Caroline Colton is easily the most interesting person in Firelight Falls.

"Unit Three, come in." The radio crackles to life with Donna's voice from dispatch.

I pick up the handset. "Unit Three here."

"Ben, your mother called the station again. Wanted me to remind you about Sunday dinner and that you need to bring someone this time. Her exact words were, 'Tell Benjamin that if he shows up alone again, I'm setting him up with Pastor Mike's niece.'"

I groan. Donna's laughter carries through the static.

"Thanks for the warning," I mutter.

"No problem, Officer Ramirez. By the way, was that Jake Colton's sister you just pulled over? Again?"

News travels at light speed in a town this size. "Just doing my job, Donna."

"Uh-huh. Your job specifically involves monitoring Maple Street, where she drives every day after work?"

I ignore that comment. "Any actual calls I should know about?"

"Nope. Quiet day in paradise. Perfect time to think about who you're bringing to Sunday dinner."

I hang up and sigh. My family's weekly Sunday dinners have become an exercise in torture since my younger sister got engaged. Now my mother has decided that at forty-two, I'm in danger of eternal bachelorhood, which is apparently a fate worse than death in the Ramirez family.

I start the cruiser and pull back onto the road, making my usual circuit through downtown. Firelight Falls is postcard-perfect in the summer, with its redbrick storefronts and hanging flower baskets. I wave at Annie through the window of her bakery as I pass; she's at the counter with my fire chief buddy Jake, her husband now. Their romance was the talk of the town last spring—the widowed fire chief and the baker finding love again after all those years apart.

I'm happy for them. I really am. But their happiness has only made my mother more determined to see me settled down too.

As I drive past the municipal building, I catch sight of Caroline again, striding up the steps in her pencil skirt and blouse, looking completely out of place among the casual summer attire of everyone else. Her dark hair is pulled back in a severe twist, and she moves with the kind of purpose rarely seen in our laid-back town.

City girl, through and through. I've heard the whispers around town—how she's just here temporarily, how she can't wait to get back to her important job in Boston. But I've seen her at town meetings, having fun at the spring festival, and she doesn't look like a woman with one foot out the door to me.

I tap my fingers on the steering wheel, thinking about my mother's ultimatum and the horror that is Pastor Mike's overeager niece, when an absolutely terrible idea begins to form.

Caroline Colton already thinks the worst of me. She says she's only here temporarily, with no desire to put down roots. And she's the last person anyone would expect me to bring to a family dinner.

It's a completely ridiculous plan. There's no way she'd ever agree to help me.

But as I circle around to the station, I can't help but smile at the thought of asking Firelight Falls' most reluctant resident to be my fake date. The worst she can do is say no.

And if there's one thing I've learned about Caroline Colton, it's that she doesn't back down.

Three

CAROLINE

The bell above Annie's Bakery chimes as I push through the door, and the smell of fresh bread and cinnamon immediately wraps around me like a hug. This is the one thing about Firelight Falls I can't complain about—Annie's coffee is better than anything I ever found in Boston.

"Caroline!" Annie's face lights up from behind the counter, her dark curls escaping from her bandana as usual. "You're early today."

"Couldn't sleep." I approach the counter, already reaching for my wallet. "Large black coffee, please."

"You know, we have pastries too. Delicious ones. Made fresh this morning by yours truly." She's already pouring my coffee, but there's something in her smile that puts me on edge. I've seen that look before. It's the same look she had right before she convinced me to enter the pie-eating contest at the spring festival.

"Just coffee, thanks."

"Suit yourself." She slides the cup across the counter, then leans forward on her elbows. "So. I was talking to Pastor Mike yesterday."

Oh no.

"His nephew is visiting for the summer. Very nice. Accountant. Stable job, good benefits—"

"Annie."

"He volunteers at the animal shelter on weekends. Loves dogs. You love dogs."

"I'm allergic to dogs."

"You could take medication." She waves her hand dismissively. "The point is, he's new in town, doesn't know anyone, and I thought maybe you could show him around. As a welcome committee. A very single welcome committee."

I take a long sip of my coffee, buying time. The problem with Annie is that she's incredible. She sits with my mom when I need a break, she brings over casseroles I pretend I don't need, and she makes Jake happier than I've ever seen him. I owe her approximately seven thousand favors.

But I do not owe her my love life.

"That's really thoughtful," I say carefully, "but I'm not looking to date anyone right now. I'm focused on Mom, and work, and—"

"You work from your laptop three days a week and spend the other two at the municipal building arguing about zoning laws for fun." Annie raises an eyebrow. "You have time."

"Zoning laws are important."

"Ben!" Annie suddenly calls out, and my stomach drops. "Ben, come here. Tell Caroline she needs to get out more."

I turn slowly, already knowing what I'll find. Sure enough, Officer Ben Ramirez is sitting at a corner table with a half-eaten muffin and a cup of coffee, watching this entire disaster unfold with undisguised amusement.

"I don't think Caroline needs my advice on her social life," he says, but he's already standing, already walking over with that easy stride that makes me want to throw my coffee at him.

"She hasn't been on a single date in years," Annie announces, as if this is a matter of public concern.

"A year and a half," I correct through gritted teeth.

"Ben, you're single. You understand. Tell her she should meet Pastor Mike's nephew."

Ben reaches the counter and stands beside me, close enough that I catch that pine scent again. He looks down at me with those dark eyes, and I can see him fighting a smile.

"I think," he says slowly, "that Caroline is perfectly capable of deciding who she wants to spend time with."

"Thank you," I say, surprised.

"Even if her choices so far have been questionable."

And there it is.

Annie sighs dramatically. "Fine. But don't come crying to me when you're forty and alone with seventeen cats."

"I'm allergic to cats too."

"Hypoallergenic cats exist, Caroline!"

Ben pulls out his wallet and hands Annie a few bills before I can protest. "Her coffee's on me today. Consider it an apology for yesterday's traffic stop."

Annie's eyes narrow, darting between us with sudden interest. "Third one this month, I heard."

"News travels fast," Ben says mildly.

"It's a small town." Annie is definitely smiling now, and I don't like it one bit. "You two have a good day."

I grab my coffee and head for the door before Annie can get any more ideas. Ben follows me out onto the sidewalk, matching my pace as I walk toward my car.

"You didn't have to do that," I say.

"Buy your coffee? Consider it a public service. You looked like you were about to commit a felony in there."

"Annie means well."

"She does." He's quiet for a moment as we reach my car. "Pastor Mike's nephew, huh?"

"Apparently, he loves dogs and has good benefits." I dig my keys out of my purse. "Lucky me."

"Yeah, about that." Ben clears his throat, and something in his tone makes me pause. "I might have a proposition for you."

I turn to face him, leaning against my car door. "A proposition."

"My mother is on the warpath. If I show up to Sunday dinner alone again, she's setting me up with Pastor Mike's niece. Who, from what I understand, has already picked out wedding venues."

"Sounds like a you problem, Officer."

"It is. But here's the thing." He takes a step closer, lowering his voice even though the sidewalk is empty. "You've got Annie trying to set you up. I've got my mother threatening to set me up. We could solve both problems at once."

It takes me a second to understand what he's saying. When I do, I actually laugh.

"You want me to be your fake girlfriend."

"Fake date," he corrects. "To Sunday dinner. Just enough to get my mother off my back. And in return, I'll make sure Annie knows we're... seeing each other. She'll back off."

"That's the most ridiculous thing I've ever heard."

"Is it?" He tilts his head, studying me. "You're a lawyer. Think of it as a contract. Mutually beneficial terms, clear exit strategy, no strings attached."

I should say no. Every logical part of my brain is screaming at me to say no. This is Ben Ramirez—the man who's pulled me over three times in a month, who looks at me like he knows exactly how much he gets under my skin, who is my brother's best friend.

"No," I say.

His expression doesn't change, but something flickers in his eyes. "Fair enough."

"It would never work. People would see right through it."

"Probably."

"And I don't even like you," I say. It's not like he has to know I've been attracted to him for a while now. Nope. I don't have room in my life for a relationship. I'll keep my heart in one piece. Thank you very much.

"The feeling is mutual, Counselor." But he's smiling now, that infuriating smile that makes me want to argue with him just for the satisfaction of it. "Forget I asked. Have a good day, Caroline."

He turns and walks away, hands in his pockets, not looking back.

I get in my car and start the engine, telling myself I made the right decision. A fake relationship with Ben Ramirez is a terrible idea. Terrible.

I'm still telling myself that when I pull into my driveway twenty minutes later and find Annie's car already there.

Four

BEN

I'M NOT SURPRISED SHE said no.

Actually, that's not true. I'm a little surprised she didn't laugh harder. Caroline Colton agreeing to pretend to date me was always a long shot—somewhere between winning the lottery and Mrs. Henderson's chicken learning to fly.

Still, it was worth a try.

I spend the morning on patrol, which in Firelight Falls means driving slowly through downtown, waving at shop owners, and breaking up an argument between two elderly men playing chess too aggressively in the park. By noon, I've made peace with my inevitable fate. Sunday dinner with Pastor Mike's niece, followed by a lifetime of my mother's disappointed sighs.

I'm parked outside the fire station, eating a sandwich and reviewing paperwork, when a sharp knock on my window nearly makes me choke on my turkey and Swiss.

Caroline Colton stands outside my cruiser, arms crossed, looking like she's about to depose a hostile witness.

I roll down the window. "Ms. Colton. Did I pull you over in my sleep?"

"We need to talk."

"We do?"

She glances around the parking lot, then back at me. "Not here. Can you take a break?"

I look at my half-eaten sandwich, then at her face—that determined set to her jaw that I'm starting to recognize as Caroline gearing up for battle.

"I can take a break," I say.

Five minutes later, we're sitting across from each other at a picnic table behind the fire station, far enough from the building that no one can overhear us. Caroline has her hands wrapped around a water bottle, her fingers tapping an anxious rhythm.

"I have conditions," she says.

I blink. "Conditions."

"For your proposal. The fake dating thing." She meets my eyes, all business. "If we're going to do this, we're going to do it right. I don't do anything halfway."

I lean back, trying not to smile. "I'm listening."

"First, we need to establish a clear timeline. We're 'dating'"—she makes air quotes—"until the end of summer. That gives us about six weeks. After that, we have an amicable breakup, no hard feelings, and everyone moves on."

"Reasonable."

"Second, we need boundaries. We hold hands in public if necessary. Maybe a kiss on the cheek for special occasions. But nothing—" She falters, and I watch a flush creep up her neck. "Nothing beyond that."

"Noted."

"Third, I will meet your family exactly three times. Sunday dinners or equivalent. I'm not spending every weekend pretending to be charmed by your relatives."

"They're very charming relatives."

"I'm sure they are. Three times."

"And last but not least, we will have up to three fake dates around town so people believe we are really dating. If we aren't seen together, Annie will never buy it."

I nod, turning over her terms in my head. They're smart. Exactly what I'd expect from a woman who spent five years handling high-stakes negotiations.

"Can I add a condition?" I ask.

Her eyes narrow. "What?"

"If we're doing this, we need to be convincing. That means you actually have to be nice to me in public. No death glares. No arguing about traffic violations. We're supposed to be falling for each other."

"I can be nice."

"Caroline. You looked at me like I was a cockroach when I bought your coffee this morning."

"That was before we had an arrangement." She tilts her chin up. "I'm an excellent actress when I need to be."

"Uh-huh." I extend my hand across the table. "So we have a deal?"

She stares at my hand for a long moment. I can practically see her running through every possible outcome, every way this could go wrong, every reason she should walk away.

Then she reaches out and shakes it, her grip firm and professional.

"Deal," she says. "But if this blows up in our faces, I'm blaming you entirely."

"Wouldn't expect anything less." I don't let go of her hand right away, and her eyes flicker with uncertainty so quickly I wonder if I imagined it. "So, fake girlfriend. What made you change your mind?"

She pulls her hand back, tucking it in her lap. "Annie was at my house when I got home. She'd already called Pastor Mike to set up a coffee date for the nephew and me. This Saturday."

"Ah."

"I told her I couldn't make it because I had plans. She asked what plans." Caroline sighs, rubbing her temple. "And I panicked and said I had a date."

"A date with whom?"

She levels me with a look that could cut glass. "Guess."

I can't help it—I laugh. A real laugh, the kind that makes her scowl deepen even as her eyes soften.

"So you told your sister-in-law that you're dating the cop who keeps pulling you over?"

"I told her I was seeing someone. She made assumptions. I didn't correct them."

"This is going to be fun."

"This is going to be a disaster," she corrects. "But at least it's a disaster of my own choosing."

I stand up from the picnic table, offering her my hand to help her up. She ignores it and stands on her own, because of course she does.

"I'll pick you up Saturday at seven," I say. "For our first official date."

"Where are we going?"

"It's a surprise."

"I hate surprises."

"I know." I grin at her, and for just a second, I see the corner of her mouth twitch like she's fighting a smile. "That's what makes it fun."

She shakes her head, but she's not scowling anymore. "Saturday at seven. Don't be late."

"Wouldn't dream of it, Counselor."

I watch her walk back to her car, and this time, I don't pretend I'm not looking.

Caroline Colton just agreed to be my fake girlfriend.

This is either the best idea I've ever had, or it's going to blow up spectacularly in my face.

Either way, I can't wait to find out.

Five

CAROLINE

BEN RAMIREZ IS EARLY.

I'm still fastening my earrings when the doorbell rings at 6:47, and my heart does a little flip that I refuse to examine too closely. I've dated plenty of men—lawyers, bankers, one memorable disaster of a surgeon—and not a single one of them ever showed up early. Five minutes late was considered punctual.

I take one last look in the mirror. I've traded my usual pencil skirt for a soft blue fitted sundress. I decided to be comfortable since Ben wouldn't give me any hints about our date. My hair is down for once, falling past my shoulders in loose waves.

"This is fake." I remind myself. *"It's a business arrangement."*

I open the door, and my carefully prepared greeting dies in my throat.

Ben Ramirez in a police uniform is annoying. Ben Ramirez in charcoal slacks and a deep green button-up, sleeves rolled to his forearms, is something else entirely. The color brings out the warmth in his skin, and without the badge and belt, he looks less like the officer who keeps pulling me over and more like someone I might actually want to spend an evening with.

"You're early," I say, because I need to say something.

"Habit." He holds up a small bouquet of wildflowers—nothing fancy, just a cheerful tumble of yellow and purple blooms. "These are for you."

I take the flowers, surprised. "You didn't have to do that."

"First date. Seemed appropriate." His eyes travel over me, an appreciative smile tugging at his too kissable lips. "You look... different."

"Different good or different bad?"

"Different—like I might have to arrest myself for staring."

I feel the heat climb up my neck and turn away to hide it, busying myself by putting the flowers in water. "Flattery won't get you out of telling me where we're going."

"It's still a surprise."

"I told you I hate surprises."

"And I told you that's what makes it fun." He's leaning against my doorframe now, completely at ease, and it irritates me how natural he looks there. "Ready?"

I grab my purse and follow him out to his truck—not the cruiser, thankfully, but a clean black pickup that suits him. He reaches the passenger door before I do and opens it, offering his hand to help me up.

"I can get into a truck by myself," I say.

"I know you can." He doesn't move his hand. "Humor me. Please?"

I take it. His palm is warm and rough against mine, and he doesn't let go until I'm settled in the seat. The door closes with a solid click, and I use the few seconds before he rounds the hood to take a breath.

Business arrangement. That's all this is.

He climbs in and starts the engine, pulling out of my driveway with the ease of someone who knows these roads like the back of his hand. The sun is just starting its descent, painting everything gold.

"You clean up well," I say, because the silence feels too charged. "I wasn't sure you owned clothes that weren't a uniform."

"I have an entire closet full. Shocking, I know."

"Do you also have a personality outside of writing traffic tickets, or is that your entire identity?"

He laughs, and it's that same warm sound that does something to my chest. "Guess you'll have to find out tonight, Counselor."

We drive for about fifteen minutes, past the downtown strip and out toward the edge of town where the buildings thin out and the trees get thicker. I'm expecting a restaurant, maybe that Italian place everyone raves about, so when he pulls into the parking lot of a converted barn with a sign that reads "Canvas & Corks," I turn to stare at him.

"A painting class?"

"Couples painting night." He cuts the engine and grins at me. "I figured if we're going to be convincing, we should have a story. 'We took a painting class together' sounds better than 'He pulled her over for speeding and they decided to fake date.'"

"I can't paint."

"Neither can I. That's the fun part."

"Ben—"

"Come on, Caroline." He's already out of the truck, coming around to open my door again. "Live a little. What's the worst that could happen?"

The worst that could happen is that I enjoy myself. The worst that could happen is that I start to think of this as something real.

But I take his hand anyway and let him help me down.

The barn has been transformed into an art studio, with easels set up in pairs and a cheerful instructor named Mallory who speaks entirely in exclamation points. There's an assortment of wine and flavored sparkling waters, and the painting we're supposed to recreate is a sunset over a lake.

"This doesn't look like a lake," Ben says twenty minutes in, squinting at his canvas. "This looks like a crime scene."

I lean over to look. He's not wrong—his lake is more of a muddy brown blob, and his sunset has the vibe of an active fire rather than a peaceful evening.

"It's abstract," I offer.

"It's terrible." But he's laughing, and so am I, and somewhere along the way I stopped keeping track of how many times our shoulders brushed or how often he leaned in to 'help' me with my technique.

"Yours isn't much better," he points out, nodding at my canvas.

"Excuse me, mine is clearly superior." I gesture at my slightly lopsided trees. "These are meant to be impressionistic."

"They're meant to be trees."

"I will throw this paintbrush at you."

"Assault on an officer. I'd have to arrest you."

"You're off duty."

"I'm never fully off duty." He dips his brush in orange paint and adds what I think is supposed to be a sun. It looks more like a basketball. "Especially when dangerous criminals like you are around."

I'm smiling. I'm genuinely smiling, and I can't remember the last time I felt this light. Not since before Mom got sick. Not since I traded my Boston apartment for my hometown and convinced myself I was fine with the change.

"You're not as annoying as I thought," I admit.

"High praise from you, Counselor." He catches my eye and winks. "You're not so bad yourself."

"Don't let it go to your head."

"Wouldn't dream of it."

Mallory calls time before I'm ready, and we step back to survey our masterpieces. They're both objectively awful, but Ben insists on taking a photo of us holding our canvases, our shoulders pressed together as he angles his phone.

"Evidence," he says. "For when people ask how we met."

"We met because this town is too small, and you kept pulling me over."

"Fine. Evidence of our first date, then."

I look at the photo on his screen—the two of us, paint-smudged and smiling, looking for all the world like a couple actually falling for each other.

"Come on," Ben says, tucking his phone away. "I promised you dinner, and there's only one place in Firelight Falls that does pizza right."

Six

BEN

She's laughing.

That's all I can think as I drive us to Sal's Pizzeria, Caroline Colton is actually laughing at something I said, and the sound is better than I imagined. It's not polite or restrained. It's real, surprised out of her like she didn't mean to let it happen.

I pull into Sal's lot and park near the entrance. The place is packed for a Saturday night, which I should have expected, but Caroline doesn't seem to mind. She's still holding her terrible painting, refusing to leave it in the truck.

"It's a memento," she says when I raise an eyebrow.

"It's evidence of a war crime against art."

"I'm keeping it forever just to spite you."

Sal's is exactly what it sounds like—a family-owned pizzeria with red-checkered tablecloths, candles in wine bottles, and the best pepperoni in the state. I guide Caroline toward a booth in the back, my hand hovering at the small of her back without quite touching.

We've just sat down, menus in hand, when I hear it.

"Ben? Caroline?"

I look up to find Annie standing at the edge of our table with a takeout bag in one hand and an expression of pure delight on her face. Jake is beside her, arms crossed, looking significantly less delighted.

"Hey, Annie." I keep my voice casual. "Jake. What are you two doing here?"

"Just grabbing dinner before we pick Maddie up from the school. She had soccer practice tonight." Jake says. "Hi Caroline, fancy seeing you here."

"Hi." Caroline's smile has gone slightly frozen. I can feel the tension radiating off her as Annie slides into the booth beside her, uninvited and clearly planning to stay.

"Jake, sit down. We're not interrupting, are we?" Annie asks, beaming.

"You're definitely interrupting," Jake says, but he slides in next to me anyway. His eyes meet mine, and there's a clear warning in them. *That's my little sister.*

I give him a small nod. *I know. I've got her.*

"So, how long have you two been sneaking around and not telling family you were dating?" She shakes her head. "And to think I was going to set you up with Pastor Mike's nephew."

Caroline glances at me, and I see the panic flickering behind her composure. This is it—the first real test. The reason we're doing this in the first place.

I reach across the table and take her hand.

Her fingers tense for just a second before she relaxes into it, and when she looks at me, her expression shifts. The panic fades, replaced by warmth. She's a better actress than I expected.

"It's new," Caroline says smoothly. "We didn't want to say anything until we knew it was... something."

"And is it?" Annie's voice is practically vibrating with excitement. "Something?"

"Yeah." I run my thumb over Caroline's knuckles, and I watch her breath catch. "I think it might be."

The words come out more honest than I intended.

"I think it's great," Annie says. "You two are perfect for each other. All that bickering? That's just tension. I said that to Jake, didn't I, honey? I said, 'Those two just need to admit they like each other.'"

"You did say that," Jake confirms. He's still watching me with that assessing look, the one I've seen him use on new recruits at the fire station. "Multiple times."

"Because I was right." Annie finally releases Caroline's arm and slides out of the booth. "We'll let you get back to your date. But I want details later, Caroline. All of them."

"There's really not much to tell—"

"All. Of. Them." Annie points at her, then at me. "Don't mess this up, Ben Ramirez."

"Wouldn't dream of it."

Jake stands, but he lingers for a moment. His hand lands on my shoulder, heavy and deliberate.

"She's been through a lot," he says quietly, just for me. "Don't make it worse."

"I won't."

He holds my gaze for a long second, then nods. Whatever he's looking for, he seems to find it. "Good. Enjoy your pizza."

They leave with their takeout, Annie still chattering excitedly as they push through the front door. The moment they're gone, Caroline lets out a breath and drops her head into her hands.

"Oh, my gosh."

"That wasn't so bad."

"Annie is going to tell everyone. By tomorrow morning, the entire town will think we're dating."

"That's... kind of the point, Caroline."

She lifts her head, and I realize I'm still holding her hand. Neither of us moves to let go.

"I know," she says. "I just didn't expect it to feel so—"

"So what?"

She shakes her head, pulling her hand back. "Nothing. Let's order. I'm starving."

But I caught the word she didn't say, because I'm thinking it too.

Real.

This is starting to feel real.

And I'm not sure if that's a problem or the best thing that's ever happened to me.

We stay at Sal's until the candles burn low and the crowd thins out. We talk about everything and nothing—her cases in Boston, my years on the force, the time I arrested Mrs. Henderson's chicken for disorderly conduct (I didn't, but Caroline laughs so hard she snorts, and I'd make up a hundred fake stories just to hear that sound again).

When I walk her to her door, she's still carrying that terrible painting.

"I had fun," she says, and she sounds almost surprised.

"Don't sound so shocked."

"I'm just saying. For a fake date, it was... nice."

"Nice." I lean against her porch railing. "I'll take it."

She hesitates at her door, keys in hand. The porch light catches the gold flecks in her eyes, and for a moment, neither of us moves.

"Saturday was a success," she says finally. "One down."

"Two to go."

"Two to go." She unlocks her door but doesn't go inside. "Thanks, Ben. For tonight."

"Anytime, Counselor."

She rolls her eyes, but she's smiling. "Goodnight."

"Goodnight, Caroline."

I wait until she's inside, until the door closes and the light flicks on in her living room. Then I walk back to my truck, my hands in my pockets, grinning like an idiot.

One fake date down.

And already, I'm counting the hours until the next one.

Seven

CAROLINE

THE DOORBELL RINGS AT seven-thirty in the morning, which is practically a home invasion.

I stumble out of bed, grab my robe, and make it to the front door just as the bell rings again. Through the peephole, I see Annie holding a bakery box and two cups of coffee, bouncing on her heels like a golden retriever who's discovered where the treats are hidden.

I open the door. "Annie. It's Sunday."

"I brought cinnamon rolls." She breezes past me into the house. "The good ones. With the cream cheese frosting."

"It's seven-thirty in the morning."

"I've been up since four. Bakers' hours." She's already in my kitchen, setting out the rolls and placing a coffee in front of my usual seat. "Sit. Eat. Talk."

I sit, because arguing with Annie is pointless when she's in interrogation mode. The coffee is perfect, and the cinnamon roll is still warm. I take a bite and try to pretend I'm not being ambushed.

"So," Annie says, settling across from me with her own coffee. "Ben Ramirez."

"What about him?"

"Caroline." She gives me the look—the one she usually reserves for customers who try to haggle over muffin prices. "I saw you two last night. The hand-holding? The way he looked at you?" She claps her hands together. "Swoon!"

I focus on my cinnamon roll. "We're just... seeing where it goes."

"Uh-huh. And where is it going?"

The honest answer is exactly three family dinners, three fake dates, and then an amicable fake breakup at the end of summer. But I can't say that. And the strange thing is, when I open my mouth to give a vague non-answer, something else comes out instead.

"I don't know," I admit. "He's not what I expected."

Annie leans forward, eyes bright. "Tell me everything."

And I do.

I tell her about the painting class, about his terrible sunset, and my lopsided trees. I tell her about the way he opened my car door without making it feel like a statement, the wildflowers he brought, how he made me laugh until my cheeks hurt. I tell her about the porch at the end of the night, the way he waited until I was inside before he left.

What I don't tell her is that it's all supposed to be pretend.

"He's good," I say, and the words feel true even though they shouldn't. "He's genuinely good, Annie. Not in that boring way where someone's nice because they don't have enough personality to be anything else. He's good in a way that makes me want to be... softer, I guess. Less guarded."

Annie reaches across the table and squeezes my hand. "That's not a bad thing, you know. Being softer."

"It feels dangerous."

"The best things usually do."

I take a sip of my coffee, avoiding her gaze. It's easier than expected to talk about Ben this way—to describe feelings I'm supposedly faking. Maybe because some part of me isn't faking at all.

But I'm not ready to examine that too closely.

"He's taking me to meet his family today," I say instead. "Sunday dinner."

Annie practically squeals. "Oh, you're going to love the Ramirezes. His mom makes the best tamales in three counties, and his dad tells the worst jokes you've ever heard. They're wonderful."

"You know them?"

"Everyone knows everyone in Firelight Falls, Caroline. Keep up." She grins. "His mom has been trying to get him married off for years. She's going to adore you."

"That's what I'm afraid of."

"Don't be." Annie stands, gathering her coffee and the now-empty bakery box. "Just be yourself. The real you—the one who argues about zoning laws and secretly loves this town even though she pretends she doesn't. Ben sees that person. His family will too."

She kisses my cheek on her way out, leaving me alone in my kitchen with the lingering scent of cinnamon and a growing knot in my stomach.

Easy peasy... I'll just... be myself. Because that's always worked in the past.

Eight

BEN

I PULL UP TO Caroline's house at exactly 4:45—fifteen minutes early, because apparently that's who I am now. A guy who shows up early with sweaty palms, nervous about introducing his fake girlfriend to his family.

Fake. Right. I need to remember that part.

She opens the door before I can knock, and for a second, I forget how to breathe. She's wearing a simple green dress that matches her eyes, her hair loose around her shoulders, and she's holding a box of cookies like a shield.

"Annie said I should bring something," she explains. "Are cookies okay? I don't know what your family likes. I almost bought flowers, but then I thought maybe your mom would think I was trying too hard."

"Caroline."

She stops. "What?"

"You're rambling."

"I don't ramble."

"You're literally rambling right now." I take the box from her hands before she can strangle it. "Cookies are perfect. My mom will love them. And you."

"You don't know that."

"I do, actually." I guide her toward the truck, opening her door because I know it annoys her and because I like the way her nose scrunches when she's trying not to smile. "You're smart, you're funny, and you'll probably end up in a debate with my dad about property taxes within the first hour. He's going to think you're the best thing that's ever happened to me."

She climbs into the truck and looks at me with an odd expression I can't quite name. "And what do you think?"

The question catches me off guard. I stand there, hand on the door, trying to find an answer that's honest without being too honest.

"I think," I say carefully, "that this is going to be an interesting evening."

I close the door before she can respond.

My parents' house is exactly what you'd expect from a couple who've been married for forty-five years—a rambling ranch-style with a garden my mother tends like it's her child and a garage my father has converted into a woodworking shop. There are cars in the driveway already. My brother Marco's SUV and my parents' ancient sedan, which Dad refuses to replace.

"Ready?" I ask as I park.

"No." Caroline smooths her dress. "But let's do it, anyway."

The front door swings open before we're halfway up the walk, and my mother appears in the doorway, arms already outstretched.

"Benjamin! You're early!" She pulls me into a hug that smells like cumin and garlic, then releases me to turn her attention to Caroline. "And you must be the woman who's finally tamed my son."

"Mom—"

"I'm Elena. Come in, come in. Marco and Sofia are already here with the baby—have you held a baby before? Lucas is three months old and an angel, except when he's not, but that's babies for you."

Caroline shoots me a look that says, "Help me," as my mother ushers her inside. I follow, already bracing for impact.

The living room is controlled chaos. My brother Marco is on the couch with his son Lucas on his shoulder, patting his back in that rhythmic way new parents master. His wife, Sofia, is in the kitchen with my father, arguing about the correct way to slice tomatoes. The TV is on, tuned to a soccer game no one is watching, and somewhere in the background, music is playing from my mother's ancient radio.

"Everyone," my mother announces, "this is Caroline. Ben's girlfriend."

The word girlfriend lands like a grenade. Marco's eyebrows shoot up. Sofia pokes her head out of the kitchen. My father sets down his knife and wipes his hands on a towel, studying Caroline with open curiosity.

"Hi," Caroline says, and I watch her lawyer composure click into place—spine straight, smile pleasant, handshake ready. "Thank you for having me."

"She brought cookies," I add, holding up the box.

"A woman with manners." My father takes the box and smiles. "I'm Roberto. That's Marco, Sofia, and the tiny one is Lucas. You play soccer?"

"I... not really?"

"Shame. We need another defender for the backyard games." He claps me on the shoulder. "Good job, mijo. She's pretty."

"Dad."

"What? I'm old. I'm allowed to state facts."

Caroline's cheeks are pink, but she's fighting a smile. My mother loops an arm through hers and steers her toward the kitchen, already launching into a detailed history of tonight's menu and why her tamales are superior to anything served at that "overpriced restaurant downtown."

Marco catches my eye and tips his head toward the back porch. I follow him out, leaving Caroline to navigate the gauntlet alone. She'll be fine. Probably.

"So," Marco says, leaning against the railing, cradling Lucas in his arms. "This is serious?"

"It's new."

"New like actually new, or new like you've been pining for years and finally made a move?" He grins at my expression. "Come on, man. She's all you've talked about for a while now. 'Jake's sister this, Jake's sister that.' You're not subtle."

"I have no idea what you're talking about."

"Sure you don't." He bounces Lucas gently as the baby fusses. "She seems good, though. Solid. Not like that last disaster you brought home."

"We don't talk about Melissa."

"We should. Just so you remember what a bad choice looks like and can appreciate a good one when you see her." He nods toward the kitchen window, where I can see Caroline laughing at something my mother said. "That one's a good one, Ben. Don't screw it up."

"Thanks for the vote of confidence."

"Anytime, little brother."

Dinner is everything I expected and more.

My mother's tamales are perfect, as always. My father tells three terrible jokes that make Caroline groan and then laugh despite herself. Sofia grills Caroline about her legal career with genuine fascination, and Marco keeps sneaking cookies while Lucas sleeps peacefully in a bassinet by the table.

Caroline fits.

That's the thing I can't stop noticing. She fits into the chaos of my family like she was always meant to be here—arguing good-naturedly with my father about local politics, complimenting my mother's cooking with obvious sincerity, letting Sofia drag her into a passionate discussion about some true-crime podcast they both love.

She's not performing. She's just... here. Present. Real.

"So, Caroline," my mother says during a lull in conversation, and I recognize the tone immediately. "Ben tells me you moved back to take care of your mother."

"That's right."

"Such a good daughter." My mother reaches over to pat Caroline's hand. "Family is everything, yes? You understand that. I can tell."

"I do," Caroline says softly. "She's... she doesn't always know who I am anymore. But she's still my mom."

My mother makes a sympathetic sound and squeezes her hand tighter. "You're a strong woman. Ben needs a strong woman."

"Mom," I warn.

"What? I'm stating facts. Like your father." She turns back to Caroline, undeterred. "You know, I'm not getting any younger. Neither is Roberto. We'd like more grandchildren before we're too old to chase them."

"Ma—"

"Lucas needs cousins, Caroline. Sofia, tell her. Doesn't Lucas need cousins?"

"He really does," Sofia says, grinning at my discomfort.

"So." My mother fixes me with a look that could pin a butterfly to a board. "When are you making this official, Benjamin? You two aren't getting any younger either."

Caroline chokes on her sweet tea. I reach over to pat her back, shooting my mother a look that she cheerfully ignores.

"We're taking things slow," I manage.

"Slow is for tortoises. You're forty-two. At your age, your father and I had been married twenty years."

"Times were different then."

"Times, schmimes." She waves her hand dismissively. "When you know, you know. And I can tell you know. Both of you." Her gaze softens as it moves between us. "A mother sees these things."

Under the table, Caroline's hand finds mine. I don't know if it's for show or for comfort, but I hold on anyway.

"We'll figure it out," I say. "I promise."

My mother looks at our joined hands and smiles—warm and knowing. "See that you do, mijo. See that you do."

Later, after coffee and my father's fourth terrible joke, we say our goodbyes. My mother hugs Caroline for a long time, whispering something in her ear that makes her laugh. My father shakes her hand and tells her she's welcome anytime. Marco claps me on the shoulder and mouths "don't screw it up" behind Caroline's back.

Sofia presses a container of leftover tamales into Caroline's hands. "For your mom," she says. "Elena's recipe. Everyone loves them."

Caroline's eyes go bright, and for a second, I think she might cry. "Thank you," she says. "Really. Thank you."

The drive back to her house is quiet. Not uncomfortable—just full. Like we're both processing something we don't have words for yet.

When I pull into her driveway, she doesn't move to get out.

"Your family is wonderful," she says finally.

"They're a lot."

"They're wonderful," she repeats. "All that chaos and noise and... love. You're lucky, Ben."

"I know."

She turns to look at me, and in the dim light from the porch, her expression is unguarded in a way I've never seen before.

"Thank you for tonight," she says. "I know it was just part of the arrangement, but... thank you."

Just part of the arrangement. Right. The arrangement.

"Caroline—"

"I should go." She grabs the tamales and her purse, fumbling for the door handle. "I'll see you around, Officer."

She's out of the truck and up the porch steps before I can figure out what I wanted to say. The door closes behind her, and I'm left sitting in the darkness, thinking about the way she laughed with my mother, the way she held my hand under the table, the way she looked at me like maybe this was starting to feel real for her too.

I think about what my mother said. When you know, you know.

And the thing is, I do know.

I know that Caroline Colton walked into my life with her speeding tickets and her sharp tongue and her guarded heart, and somewhere along the way, she stopped being a convenient arrangement and started being the person I want to wake up next to every morning.

I know that our deal has an expiration date—six weeks. End of summer. Amicable breakup, no strings attached.

I know that if I don't find a way to change the terms of our contract, I'm going to lose her.

And I know, with a certainty that settles into my bones like a promise, that I'm not willing to let that happen.

Now, I just have to convince her.

Nine

CAROLINE

I'M STANDING AT PUMP three, watching the numbers climb on the gas meter, when a familiar black truck pulls into the station.

No. No, no, no.

I consider abandoning my half-filled tank and making a run for it, but that would be ridiculous. I'm a grown woman. A lawyer. I don't flee from gas stations because of inconvenient men.

Ben parks at pump four—right next to me, because of course he does—and climbs out of his truck. He's in jeans and a faded t-shirt, off-duty, which means he has all the time in the world for this conversation.

"Caroline." He nods like this is perfectly normal. Like we're just two people who happened to need gas at the same time. "Fancy meeting you here."

"Ben." I grip the pump handle tighter and stare determinedly at the numbers ticking upward. Maybe if I don't make eye contact, he'll go away.

He doesn't go away.

Instead, he leans against his truck, arms crossed, watching me with that infuriating patience of his. I can feel his gaze on the side of my face like a caress.

"You've been avoiding me," he says.

I have been avoiding him ever since Sunday dinner, when I felt like I was in some alternate universe where families stay together and love each other forever. I got freaked out. The longing I felt to fit in. To have that for myself. It shook me to the core. I've been taking alternate routes to the municipal building, ducking into shops when I see his cruiser, and generally behaving like a coward.

"I haven't been avoiding you," I lie. "I've been busy."

"Busy avoiding me."

"Busy with work."

"You work from your laptop three days a week." He's quoting Annie now, which means they've been talking, which means I'm going to have words with my sister-in-law. "Caroline. We had a deal."

"I'm aware of our deal."

The pump clicks off, tank full, but I don't move to put it away. That would mean turning around and facing him properly, and I'm not ready for that.

"So what's going on?" His voice is softer now, less teasing. "Did I do something wrong?"

"You didn't do anything wrong."

"Then why are you running?"

The question hits too close to home. I finally turn to face him, and he's looking at me with those dark eyes, concern written all over his face. He's not angry. He's not pushy. He's just... worried.

It would be easier if he were angry.

"I'm not running," I say, but even I can hear how unconvincing it sounds.

"You're trapped at a gas pump right now because you didn't see my truck until it was too late." A small smile tugs his lips upward, making me wonder if they are as soft as they look. "That's pretty close to running."

"That's not—" I stop. Take a breath. "Fine. Maybe I've been... creating some distance."

"Why?"

Because Sunday dinner felt too real. Because your family already treats me like I belong. "Because we are only fake dating, remember? Running into you all over town wasn't part of the deal."

"Part of that deal is being seen together. Building the story." He straightens up, tucking his thumbs into his belt. "Which is why I'm formally requesting your presence at a picnic. Tomorrow evening. Town park. Very public."

"A picnic."

"Lemonade, sandwiches, the whole thing. I'll even bring a blanket."

"You're asking me on a date while I'm trapped at a gas pump?"

"I'm asking my fake girlfriend to fulfill the terms of our arrangement." But his voice is softer now, and something in his expression makes my chest tight. "Come on, Counselor. One picnic. We'll wave at some neighbors, establish our narrative, and you can go back to avoiding me afterward if you want."

I should say no. I should tell him that Sunday dinner was too much, that his family was too wonderful, that sitting at that table pretending to be his girlfriend made me forget I was pretending at all.

But I look at him—at his ridiculous grin and his earnest eyes and the way he's standing there like he's got all the time in the world—and I hear myself say, "Fine. But I'm bringing the lemonade."

His smile widens. "Deal. Tomorrow at six. Wear something you don't mind getting grass stains on."

"Why would I get grass stains?"

"It's a park, Caroline. Things happen."

He tips an imaginary hat, climbs back into his truck, and pulls out of the station with a wave. I stand there watching his taillights disappear, the gas pump still in my hand, already looking forward to a date with a man I have no business wanting.

Ten

BEN

She shows up in a yellow sundress and sandals, carrying a pitcher of lemonade like it's a peace offering.

I've already scoped out a shady patch near the duck pond where half the town walks their dogs in the evening. Maximum visibility, like I promised. I've got a blanket spread out, a cooler full of sandwiches and fruit, and a growing suspicion that this stopped being about the arrangement somewhere around the second time she laughed at my jokes.

"You came," I say as she approaches.

"I said I would." She sets down the lemonade and surveys the setup. "This is nice."

"I made sandwiches."

"You have cloth napkins."

"My mother would disown me if I used paper." I pat the blanket beside me. "Sit. Enjoy. Pretend you like me."

She sits, tucking her legs beneath her, and I try not to notice how the sunlight catches the gold in her hair or the way her dress pools around her like a painting.

"So," she says, reaching for a sandwich. "What's the strategy here? Who are we trying to impress?"

"Everyone. Anyone." I shrug. "Mrs. Patterson walks her poodle past here every evening at six-fifteen. The Hendersons bring their grandkids to feed the ducks around six-thirty. If we're lucky, we'll get a wave from Mayor Thompson on his evening jog."

"You've really thought this through."

"I'm a man with a plan, Counselor."

She takes a bite of her sandwich and makes a small sound of approval that does things to my heart rate. "Turkey and avocado?"

"With that spicy mayo from the deli. Annie mentioned you liked it."

"You asked Annie about my sandwich preferences?" she asks, a look of surprise on her face.

"I'm thorough."

"You're something, all right."

We eat in comfortable silence for a while, watching the ducks paddle across the pond. Mrs. Patterson appears right on schedule, her poodle prancing at the end of a pink leash, and I wave. She waves back, then does a double-take when she spots Caroline beside me. I can practically see her reaching for her phone to spread the news.

"She's definitely texting someone right now," Caroline observes.

"Probably the entire garden club."

"Is that a good thing?"

"For our purposes? Absolutely." I pour two glasses of lemonade and hand her one. "By tomorrow morning, the whole town will know we had a romantic picnic by the duck pond."

"Romantic." She raises an eyebrow. "Is that what this is?"

"It's a picnic at sunset with lemonade and fancy sandwiches. If that's not romantic, I don't know what is."

She opens her mouth to respond—probably with something cutting and clever that would make me like her even more—when a voice shouts, "HEADS UP!" from somewhere behind us.

I turn just in time to see a frisbee sailing directly toward our blanket.

What happens next unfolds in slow motion. I lunge for Caroline, trying to shield her from the incoming projectile. She lurches sideways, lemonade sloshing. The frisbee clips the edge of the pitcher, which tips spectacularly, and suddenly there's lemonade everywhere—on the blanket, on the sandwiches, and most dramatically, all down the front of Caroline's yellow sundress.

A kid—maybe ten years old, mortified—skids to a stop at the edge of our blanket. "I'm so sorry! I'm so, so sorry! I didn't mean to! It got away from me."

I'm already grabbing napkins, my heart sinking. This is a disaster. Caroline is going to kill me. She's going to call off our arrangement, file a restraining order, and tell everyone in Firelight Falls that I'm an incompetent disaster of a human being who can't even plan a simple picnic without—

Caroline laughs... bright and surprised and so genuine that it stops me mid-napkin-grab.

"Oh my gosh," she says, looking down at her soaked dress. "I look like I lost a fight with a lemon tree."

"I'm so sorry," the kid says again, looking like he might cry.

Caroline waves him off, still laughing. "It's fine. Really. It's just lemonade." She looks at me, her eyes dancing. "Did you see your face? You looked like someone had just committed a felony."

"Destruction of private property," I manage. "Your dress—"

"It's a fifteen-dollar sundress from Target that's been through worse." She accepts the napkins I'm still holding and dabs at her skirt halfheartedly. "Besides, this is way more memorable than a perfect picnic. 'Remember that time a frisbee attacked us at the duck pond' is a much better story."

The kid retrieves his frisbee and scampers back to his friends, relief flooding his face. I sit there on the lemonade-damp blanket, watching Caroline Colton laugh off what should have been a disaster, and feel something in my chest crack wide open.

This is who she is, I realize. Underneath the lawyer armor and the guarded walls and the careful distance she keeps between herself and everyone else. This is the real Caroline—the one who laughs when things go wrong, who cares more about a scared kid's feelings than her ruined dress, who sits in soggy grass and makes jokes instead of storming off.

This is the woman I'm falling in love with.

"You're staring," she says.

"Sorry." I'm not sorry at all. "You're just... not what I expected."

"What did you expect?"

"Someone who'd be angry. Someone who'd blame me for the frisbee, even though it clearly wasn't my fault."

"It was definitely your fault." But she's smiling. "You picked the spot. You planned the picnic. You manifested the frisbee with your chaotic energy."

"My chaotic energy."

"It's a thing. I've observed it." She wrings out a napkin and tosses it at me. "We should probably salvage what we can. I think the grapes survived."

We spend the next few minutes picking through the wreckage, laughing at the soggy sandwiches and the lemonade-soaked blanket. The sun starts to set, painting everything gold and pink, and when Caroline leans back on her hands and tilts her face toward the sky, she looks so beautiful it almost hurts.

"Thank you," she whispers.

"For ruining your dress?"

"For making me laugh." She turns to look at me, and there's something unguarded in her expression—something vulnerable and real. "I haven't laughed like that in a long time. Not since before..."

She doesn't finish, but she doesn't have to. I know what she means. Before her mom got sick. Before she gave up her life in Boston. Before she convinced herself that joy was something she'd traded away for responsibility.

"You deserve to laugh," I tell her. "Every day. Someone should make sure of that."

"Is that an offer, Officer Ramirez?"

"Maybe it is, Counselor."

We look at each other for a long moment, the fading sunlight warm on our faces. I want to kiss her. I want to close the distance between us and find out if her lips taste like lemonade. I want to tell her that this stopped being fake for me a long time ago.

But she's not ready. I can see it in the way she pulls back just slightly, the way her guard slides back into place.

"We should probably head out," she says. "Before we attract any more frisbees."

"Probably."

I help her pack up the remains of our picnic, and we walk back to our cars in comfortable silence. She's still damp, still grass-stained, still the most beautiful thing I've ever seen.

"Same time next week?" I ask as she reaches her sedan.

"You want to do this again?"

"The part where we had fun, not the part where you got attacked by flying sports equipment."

"Fair enough." She opens her car door, then pauses. "Maybe somewhere indoors next time. Just to be safe."

"I'll take that under advisement."

She slides into her car, but before she closes the door, she looks up at me with a small smile. "Tonight was good, Ben. Really."

"Yeah," I say. "It was."

I watch her drive away, and for the second time this week, I'm left standing in the twilight, absolutely certain of two things.

One: I am completely, hopelessly in love with Caroline Colton.

Two: I have no idea how to tell her.

But I'm going to figure it out.

Because a woman who laughs in the face of flying frisbees and lemonade catastrophes is worth fighting for.

Eleven

CAROLINE

THE FIRST TEXT COMES on Monday morning.

Ben: Mrs. Henderson's chicken made another break for it. Currently negotiating a standoff behind the post office.

I'm sitting at my laptop, halfway through a contract review, and I laugh out loud before I can stop myself.

Caroline: Is this what my tax dollars pay for?

Ben: You're welcome for my service.

Ben: [photo of a very smug-looking chicken perched on a mailbox]

Caroline: She looks unrepentant.

Ben: She's a repeat offender. I'm considering pressing charges.

Caroline: I'll represent her. Pro bono.

Ben: Of course you will.

I set down my phone and try to focus on the contract, but I'm smiling for the next hour.

• • • • • • • • • • •

By Wednesday, texting Ben has become the highlight of my day.

I don't know how it happened. One minute I was avoiding him, and the next I'm checking my phone every time it buzzes, hoping it's him.

Ben: Quiet day. Helped Mr. Garcia jump his truck. Broke up a fight between two squirrels over a French fry.

Caroline: The squirrel beat should really be its own department.

Ben: I'll suggest it at the next budget meeting.

Caroline: I'll draft the proposal. "Rodent Conflict Resolution Unit."

Ben: You're hired.

That night, I'm eating leftovers when another text comes through.

Ben: How's your mom today?

Something in my chest loosens. He asks this every day now. Not in a prying way, just checking in. Like he actually wants to know.

Caroline: Good day. She remembered my name. She let me do her hair.

Ben: That's great, Caroline.

Caroline: It is. Thanks for asking.

Ben: Always.

I stare at that word for longer than I should.

• • • • • • • • • • •

Thursday brings a photo of Donna glaring at Ben over a stack of paperwork, captioned "Someone didn't appreciate my suggestion that we get an office mascot."

Friday is a voice memo of him singing along to the radio—badly—that makes me laugh until I cry.

On Saturday, he calls instead of texting.

"My parents invited us to a Rangers game tomorrow," he says without preamble. "They've got a suite. I know it's probably not your scene, but—"

"I'm in."

"Really?" He sounds shocked.

"Is that surprising?"

"I just figured... you don't seem like the sports type. No offense."

"Ben." I lean back on my couch, grinning at the ceiling. "I grew up in Texas. My dad took Jake and me to Rangers games every summer until he left. I can recite the 2010 World Series roster from memory."

"You're kidding."

"Josh Hamilton, Michael Young, Ian Kinsler—"

"Okay, okay, I believe you." He's laughing now, that warm sound I'm starting to crave. "I keep underestimating you."

"Most people do."

"I won't make that mistake again, Counselor."

We talk for another hour about nothing—favorite players, the worst stadium food, the time Jake caught a foul ball and refused to share it with me for a full year. By the time I hang up, my cheeks hurt from smiling.

This is dangerous, I think. This is starting to feel like something real.

But I don't stop smiling.

Twelve

BEN

She knows baseball.

Not just knows it—loves it. The way some people love art or music or good wine, Caroline Colton loves America's pastime. And watching her in my parents' suite, perched on the edge of her seat with a hot dog in one hand and her eyes locked on the field, is doing things to my heart I'm not prepared for.

"He should've bunted," she says, gesturing at the batter with her hot dog. "Runner on second, no outs—you move him over."

"That's what I said!" My father slaps the arm of his chair. "Elena, you hear this? The woman understands sacrifice bunts."

"She's perfect," my mother says, patting Caroline's knee. "Ben, why didn't you bring her around sooner?"

"We've only been dating a few weeks, Ma."

"A few weeks is enough." She hands Caroline a napkin. "Mustard, mija. On your chin."

Caroline wipes her chin without a trace of embarrassment, and I watch my mother beam at her like she's already part of the family.

This was supposed to be a performance. Another outing for believability, another checkmark on our arrangement. But Caroline hasn't looked at me once like she's playing a role. She's just... here. Cheering when the Rangers score, groaning at bad calls, explaining infield fly rules to my mother with the patience of a saint.

"You okay?" she asks, catching me staring.

"Yeah." I shake my head. "Just surprised, I guess."

"That I know baseball?"

"That you—" I stop myself. You keep getting better every time I think I've figured you out. "That you're having fun."

She tilts her head, something soft in her expression. "Why wouldn't I be?"

"I don't know. I thought maybe this was too..." I search for the right word, coming up blank.

"Too what? Too normal? Too real?" She bumps her shoulder against mine. "I like your parents, Ben. I like baseball. I'm allowed to enjoy myself."

"You are," I agree. "I like seeing you enjoy yourself."

Her cheeks flush, and she turns back to the game, but she doesn't move away. Her shoulder stays pressed against mine for the rest of the inning.

It happens during the seventh-inning stretch.

We're on our feet, singing "Take Me Out to the Ballgame" along with thirty thousand other fans. Caroline's got her arm looped through my mother's, both of them swaying and singing completely off-key, and I'm watching her instead of the jumbotron like an absolute fool.

Which is why I don't notice at first.

"Oh, my gosh." My mother stops singing. "Ben. Benjamin. Look."

I turn toward the massive screen just as the heart-shaped frame settles over our suite. Over me. Over Caroline.

KISS CAM, the screen announces in giant letters, and thirty thousand people start cheering.

Caroline freezes beside me. Her eyes go wide, and I watch the flush climb up her neck as she realizes what's happening.

"We don't have to." I start.

"Everyone's watching," she whispers.

"I know. It's fine. We can just wave it off."

"Ben." She grabs my shirt and pulls me toward her. "Shut up."

And then she kisses me.

It's supposed to be for show. A quick peck for the cameras, something to satisfy the crowd and my parents and whatever story we're supposed to be selling. But the moment her lips touch mine, something short-circuits in my brain.

She tastes like ballpark mustard and nachos and something sweet underneath, and her hand is fisted in my shirt like she's afraid I'll pull away. I'm not pulling away. I couldn't pull away if the stadium caught fire.

My hand finds the curve of her waist. She makes a small sound of surprise against my mouth, and I feel it in my spine. The crowd is roaring, or maybe that's just the blood in my ears, and I don't care about any of it because Caroline Colton is kissing me and it's nothing like I imagined.

It's better.

When we finally break apart, her eyes are dazed and her lips are slightly swollen, and she's looking at me like she's never seen me before.

"Wow," my mother says from somewhere behind us. "Roberto, did you see that? That was a movie kiss. That was a Telenovela kiss."

"I saw it, Elena. The whole stadium saw it."

Caroline drops her forehead to my shoulder, and I feel her laughing—or maybe hyperventilating. It's hard to tell.

"Your family is insane," she mumbles into my shirt.

"I know." I wrap my arm around her, holding her steady. My heart is pounding so hard I'm sure she can feel it. "Sorry."

She lifts her head and grins. "Don't be."

We don't talk about the kiss for the rest of the game. But she doesn't move away from me either. Her shoulder stays pressed against mine, and twice I catch her touching her lips, like she's checking to make sure it really happened.

It happened.

And I have no idea what it means.

We stay until the last out, until the Rangers win by two runs and my father has recapped every play to anyone who will listen. My mother makes Caroline promise to come to the next game, and the next one after that, and Caroline agrees with a warmth that doesn't sound forced.

On the drive home, the kiss sits between us like a third passenger.

"Thank you," she says finally.

"For what?"

"For inviting me." She looks at me, and there's something vulnerable in her expression. "For seeing me as more than just... what people expect."

I reach over and take her hand. She doesn't pull away.

"Caroline, you're the most unexpected person I've ever met. In the best way."

She's quiet for a moment, her fingers curling around mine. "This week—the texts, the calls—it was nice."

"Just nice?"

"Really nice." She squeezes my hand. "I missed you. Which is stupid, because it's only been a week, and this isn't even real, but—"

"It feels real."

She looks at me, startled.

"Doesn't it?" I press. "The texts. Tonight. My parents." I pause. "That kiss."

She pulls her hand back, and I feel the loss immediately.

"The kiss was for the camera," she says. "It had to look convincing."

"Did it?"

She doesn't answer. But I see her touch her lips again, and I know she felt it too.

We drive the rest of the way in silence, but it's not comfortable anymore. It's the kind of silence that feels like standing on the edge of something—waiting for the other person to jump first, terrified they won't.

I walk her to her door, and she pauses with her key in the lock.

"One more date, and one more family dinner," she says quietly. "That was the deal."

"I remember."

"And then we're done."

The words land like a punch. "If that's what you want."

She's quiet for a long moment, staring at her keys. When she looks up, her eyes are unreadable.

"Goodnight, Ben."

"Goodnight, Caroline."

She disappears inside, and I stand on her porch for a full minute, the ghost of her lips still burning on mine.

Thirteen

CAROLINE

I CHANGE MY OUTFIT three times before admitting I'm being ridiculous.

It's just a barbecue. Just burgers and fireworks and Ben's family, who I've already met twice and who—against all odds—seem to genuinely like me. There's no reason to be nervous.

Except this is the last one.

Family dinner number three. After today, I've fulfilled my end of the bargain. One more town date, and then we stage our amicable breakup and go back to being strangers who wave politely when we pass each other on Main Street.

The thought makes my chest ache in a way I refuse to examine.

I settle on a white sundress with tiny red flowers—festive without trying too hard—and leave my hair down because Ben mentioned once that he liked it that way. Not that it matters what Ben likes. Not that I've been cataloging every offhand comment he's made about my appearance like some lovesick teenager.

My phone buzzes.

Ben: On my way. Fair warning: my mother has been cooking since 5 am. There will be enough food for a small army.

Caroline: I'll pace myself.

Ben: That's what they all say. No one escapes Elena Ramirez's kitchen without a food coma.

I'm smiling at my phone like an idiot when he pulls into the driveway. I grab my purse and the fruit salad I made—Annie's recipe, though I'll never admit it—and head outside before he can come to the door.

He's leaning against his truck in jeans and a soft blue t-shirt that stretches across his shoulders in a way that should be illegal. When he sees me, his expression shifts into something warm and unguarded that makes my heart stutter.

"You look nice," he says.

"It's just a sundress."

"It's a nice sundress." He takes the fruit salad from my hands and opens the passenger door. "Ready for round three?"

"As ready as I'll ever be."

The drive to his parents' house is filled with easy conversation—he tells me about his latest scheme to convince Donna to adopt an office cat. I tell him about the zoning dispute that's been consuming my week. It feels natural. Comfortable. Like we've been doing this for years instead of weeks.

That's the problem. It feels too real.

When we pull up to the house, the driveway is already packed. Marco's SUV is there, along with several other cars I don't recognize. Red, white, and blue streamers hang from the porch, and I can hear music and laughter drifting from the backyard.

"Extended family," Ben explains, catching my expression. "The Fourth is kind of a big deal for the Ramirezes."

"You didn't mention there'd be extended family."

"Didn't I?" He's already out of the truck, coming around to open my door. "Must have slipped my mind."

"Ben—"

"Relax, Counselor." He offers me his hand, and I take it without thinking. "They're going to love you. Everyone loves you."

"That's not—" I start, but I don't get to finish because Elena Ramirez has appeared on the porch, arms outstretched, already calling my name.

"Caroline! Mija, you came!" She pulls me into a hug that smells like grilled onions and dessert. "Ben said you might be too busy with work, but I told him, 'Caroline is family now. She'll be here.'"

Family. The word lands like a stone in my stomach.

"I wouldn't miss it," I manage.

"Of course you wouldn't. Come, come. Everyone wants to meet Ben's girlfriend."

She loops her arm through mine and steers me toward the backyard before I can protest. Ben follows with the fruit salad, shooting me an apologetic look that I pretend not to see.

The backyard is chaos in the best possible way. Kids are running through a sprinkler, shrieking with delight. A group of older men are clustered around an enormous grill, arguing in rapid Spanish. Marco is tossing a football with a teenager who must be a cousin, while Sofia sits in a lawn chair with Lucas on her lap, chatting with a group of women who all have Elena's eyes.

"Everyone!" Elena claps her hands. "This is Caroline. Ben's girlfriend. The lawyer."

Two dozen faces turn toward me. I feel like a specimen under a microscope.

"She's pretty," announces an elderly woman in a lawn chair—Ben's grandmother, I'm guessing, based on the way everyone defers to her. "Good hips. She'll give you strong babies."

"Abuela," Ben groans from somewhere behind me.

"What? I'm old. I say what I think." She waves me over imperiously. "Come here, girl. Let me look at you."

I spend the next hour being passed from relative to relative like an interesting artifact. I meet Ben's aunts and uncles, his cousins, his grandmother, who pinches my cheeks and declares me "acceptable," and approximately seven children whose names I immediately forget.

Through it all, Ben stays close—a hand on my back, a whispered explanation of who's who, a rescue when his great-aunt tries to show me pictures of him as a naked toddler.

"Sorry," he murmurs as he steers me toward the drink table. "I should have warned you about the full Ramirez experience."

"It's fine." And strangely, it is. Despite the chaos and the overwhelming number of new faces, I feel welcome. Like I belong here. "Your family is wonderful."

"They're a lot."

"They're wonderful," I repeat. "You're lucky to have them."

He looks at me with an expression that almost seems like longing. "Yeah. I am."

Fourteen

BEN

She fits.

That's all I can think as I watch Caroline navigate my family's chaos with a grace that shouldn't surprise me anymore. She debates immigration policy with my uncle Hector, compliments my cousin Maria's quinceañera photos, and lets my grandmother teach her the "correct" way to season carne asada, even though Abuela's secret is just salt and love.

She's not performing. She's not counting down the minutes until she can leave. She's enjoying herself.

And in a few hours, this will all be over.

"You're staring again, mijo."

I turn to find my mother beside me, holding two cold bottles of water. She hands me one and tips her chin toward Caroline, who's now letting my youngest cousin show her how to do a cartwheel.

"She's something," I say.

"She is." My mother takes a sip of her beer. "So why do you look like someone canceled Christmas?"

"I don't—"

"Benjamin." She gives me the look—the one that's been making me confess my sins since I was five years old. "I'm your mother. I know when something's wrong."

I watch Caroline attempt a cartwheel and fail spectacularly, laughing as my cousin tries to correct her form. "It's complicated."

"Love usually is."

"Who said anything about love?"

My mother just smiles. "Mijo, you've brought exactly three women to meet this family in forty-two years. The first time, you were sixteen, and she broke up with you a week later. The second one was wrong for you, and everyone knew it except you. And now there's Caroline."

"What about Caroline?"

"She's different." My mother's voice softens. "She looks at you like you hung the moon. And you look at her like she's the reason the moon exists."

"Ma—"

"I'm not finished." She sets down her beer and takes my face in her hands, the way she used to when I was a kid. "Whatever is complicated, uncomplicate it. A woman like that doesn't come around twice."

She releases me and walks away before I can respond, leaving me with a half-empty bottle of water and a chest full of words I don't know how to say.

The sun sets in a blaze of orange and pink, and the family migrates to the open field behind the house for fireworks. Someone's set up lawn chairs and blankets, and coolers full of drinks are scattered across the grass.

I find Caroline standing at the edge of the crowd, a sparkler in her hand, watching my cousins chase each other with fountains of light.

"Hey," I say, coming up beside her.

"Hey yourself." She doesn't look at me, but she shifts closer, her shoulder brushing mine. "Your mom cornered me earlier."

"Uh oh. What did she say?"

"She gave me her tamale recipe." Caroline's voice is strange—thick, almost.

My heart clenches. "Caroline—"

"And your grandmother told me I should start taking prenatal vitamins. 'To be prepared,' apparently."

"I'm so sorry. I'll talk to them—"

"Don't." She finally looks at me, and there's something in her eyes I've never seen before. Something vulnerable and scared and maybe, if I'm not imagining it, hopeful. "They're wonderful, Ben. All of them. I just..."

"Just what?"

The first firework explodes overhead, a shower of red and gold that illuminates her face. She's beautiful. She's always been beautiful, but right now, lit up by the explosions in the sky, she looks like something out of a dream.

"I don't want to hurt them," she says quietly. "When this ends."

When. Not if. My stomach knots in dread.

"Caroline—"

Another firework goes off, then another, a cascade of color that drowns out whatever I was going to say. Around us, people are cheering, kids are screaming with delight, and my family is pressed together on blankets, celebrating the way they always do.

And I'm standing here, watching the woman I love prepare to walk away.

"I should—" she starts.

I take her hand.

She freezes, her eyes darting to mine. The fireworks paint shadows across her face—blue, then white, then red.

"Stay," I say. "Just... stay. Watch the fireworks with me."

She doesn't answer. But she doesn't let go either.

We stand there, hand in hand, as the sky explodes above us. She leans into my shoulder, and I feel her exhale—a long, slow release of tension that makes me wonder what she's letting go of.

"Ben," she whispers, so quiet I almost miss it under the boom of the finale.

"Yeah?"

But the last firework explodes, a massive burst of red, white, and blue that lights up the entire field, and whatever she was going to say is lost in the thunder of applause.

When the smoke clears, she pulls her hand back.

"We should head back," she says. "Help clean up."

"Caroline, wait."

But she's already walking toward the house, her white dress ghostly in the darkness.

I stand there for a long moment, watching her go.

One more date. That's all we have left. One more date, and then she's gone.

Unless I do something about it.

· · · ● · ● · ● · · ·

The drive home is quiet. Caroline stares out the window, her hands folded in her lap, her face unreadable.

"Thank you for coming," I say as I pull into her driveway.

"Thank you for inviting me." She reaches for the door handle, then pauses. "Ben..."

"Yeah?"

She turns to look at me, and for a second, I think she's going to tell me she doesn't want this to end.

"Your family is wonderful," she says instead. "You're really lucky."

"I know."

"Goodnight, Ben."

"Goodnight, Caroline."

She slips out of the truck and walks to her door. I wait until she's inside, until the light comes on in her living room, before I put the truck in reverse.

My mother's voice echoes in my head. Whatever is complicated, uncomplicate it.

She's right. She's always right.

But first, I need a plan.

Because I'm not letting Caroline Colton walk away without a fight.

Fifteen

CAROLINE

I AVOID HIM FOR 5 days.

It's not hard. I know his patrol schedule by now—an embarrassing admission I'll never make out loud—so I know which routes to take and which times to stay off the roads. I work from home instead of the municipal building. I skip my morning coffee at Annie's and make do with the ancient Keurig in my kitchen.

I tell myself it's fine. That I just need space to think.

But every time my phone buzzes, my heart leaps into my throat, and when it's not Ben, something in my chest deflates like a punctured balloon.

Even though I'm not responding, he texts me anyway.

Ben: Donna says hi. She also says you're a coward for not coming by the station.

Ben: She didn't actually say that. But she was thinking it.

Ben: Okay, maybe that was me thinking it.

Ben: I'm kidding. Sort of.

Ben: How's your mom today?

Of course, he still asks about my mom. Of course, he's still thoughtful and kind and everything I never knew I wanted until he pulled me over for speeding and ruined my entire life.

I don't respond.

On the fifth day, my phone rings. His name flashes on the screen, and I stare at it for three rings before I answer.

"Hey," I say, trying to sound casual.

"Hey yourself." His voice is warm but careful. "You've been quiet."

"Busy week."

"Right." A pause. "So, I was thinking about our last date. There's this new Italian place over in—"

"Ben." I close my eyes. "I don't think we should do the last date."

Silence. When he speaks again, his voice has lost its warmth. "What?"

"Our time is almost up anyway. We've done what we needed to do—Annie's stopped trying to set me up, your mom seems satisfied. There's no point in dragging it out."

"No point." He repeats the words like they're in a foreign language.

"It's just... it would be easier this way." I'm gripping my phone so hard my knuckles are white. "A clean break. We can tell people it just didn't work out. No hard feelings."

"Caroline—"

"We always knew this was temporary." My voice sounds steady, which is a miracle, because inside I'm falling apart. "I think it's better if we end it now. Before..."

"Before what?"

Before I fall any deeper. Before I forget, this was never real. Before I let myself believe I could have this—have him—and then lose it anyway.

"Before it gets complicated," I finish.

Another silence, longer this time. I can hear him breathing, can picture him standing somewhere with his jaw tight and his eyes that impossible shade of brown.

"Is that what you want?" he asks finally. "Really?"

No. Absolutely not. What I want is to take back every word I just said. What I want is to drive to wherever he is and tell him that somewhere between the painting class and the lemonade disaster and the kiss at the baseball game, I fell in love with him. What I want is to stop being so terrified of getting hurt that I hurt us both instead.

But I've spent my whole life protecting myself. Building walls. Keeping people at arm's length so they can't leave the way my father left, the way Jake left, the way everyone eventually leaves.

Ben Ramirez makes me want to tear those walls down, and that scares me more than anything.

"Yes," I lie. "It's what I want."

"Okay." His voice is flat now. Empty. "If that's what you want, Caroline, I'm not going to push. That's not who I am."

"I know."

"But I need you to know—" He stops. Starts again. "Never mind. It doesn't matter."

"Ben—"

"Take care of yourself, Counselor."

The line goes dead.

I sit there, phone in my hand, staring at the wall. I should feel relieved. This is what I wanted—a clean ending, no messy feelings, no risk of getting my heart broken by a man who was only ever pretending to want me.

Instead, I feel like I've made the worst mistake of my life.

Sixteen

BEN

I DON'T REMEMBER DRIVING to the station.

One minute I'm standing in my kitchen, phone in hand, listening to Caroline Colton systematically dismantle everything we built over the past few weeks. The next minute, I'm at my desk, staring at a stack of paperwork I can't process because her voice keeps echoing in my head.

Our time is almost up anyway.

No point in dragging it out.

It's what I want.

"You look like someone ran over your dog." Donna appears at the edge of my desk, coffee in hand. "What happened?"

"Nothing."

"Uh-huh." She sets the coffee in front of me. "Does 'nothing' have a law degree?"

I don't answer. I can't. If I open my mouth, I might say something I'll regret—like the fact that I'm in love with a woman who just made it very clear she doesn't feel the same way.

"Ben." Donna's voice softens. "Talk to me."

"She ended it." The words come out rough, scraped from somewhere deep. "Said there was no point in continuing. That we should just call it."

"And you let her?"

"What was I supposed to do? Force her to keep seeing me?" I shove back from my desk, pacing the small space. "She said it's what she wants. I'm not going to be the guy who can't take no for an answer."

"There's a difference between not taking no for an answer and fighting for someone who's scared."

I stop pacing. "What?"

Donna sighs, lowering herself into the chair across from my desk. "I've been married for thirty-two years, Ben. You know what I've learned? People don't always say what they mean. Especially when they're terrified of getting hurt."

"She sounded pretty sure."

"Did she? Or did she sound like someone who's spent her whole life waiting for the other shoe to drop?"

I think about Caroline. About the walls she keeps around herself, the way she deflects with sarcasm, the fear I sometimes catch flickering behind her eyes before she buries it.

"She's been through a lot," I say slowly. "Her mom's illness. Giving up her career in Boston. She doesn't let people in easily."

"And you got in." Donna raises an eyebrow. "Maybe that's exactly what scared her."

"So what am I supposed to do? Chase after her? Grand gesture, my way into her heart?"

"I don't know. That's up to you." She stands, patting my shoulder as she passes. "But I'll tell you this... if you let her walk away without at least telling her how you feel, you'll regret it for the rest of your life."

She leaves me alone with my cold coffee and my racing thoughts.

I think about the way Caroline laughed at the duck pond, lemonade dripping down her dress. The way she fit into my family like she'd always been there. The way she kissed me at the baseball game—like someone who meant it.

She said she wanted to end it.

But her voice shook when she said it.

I pull out my phone and stare at her contact. My thumb hovers over the call button.

And then I put the phone away.

If Caroline needs space, I'll give her space. If she needs time, I'll give her time. But I'm not giving up. Not yet.

First, I need to figure out what I'm going to say.

· · · ● · ● · ● · ·

The next few days are torture.

I go through the motions—patrol, paperwork, Mrs. Henderson's chicken making another break for freedom—but everything feels muted, like I'm watching my life from the outside.

Jake finds me on Thursday, parked outside the fire station during my lunch break.

"Hey." He slides into the passenger seat of my cruiser without asking. "We need to talk."

"I'm fine."

"You're not fine. You look like garbage, and my sister's been crying into her cereal for three days." He fixes me with a look that's part concern, part warning. "What happened?"

"She ended it."

"Why?"

"Said there was no point in continuing." I stare out the windshield, unable to meet his eyes. "Said it was what she wanted."

"And you believed her?"

"She was pretty convincing."

Jake is quiet for a long moment. When he speaks again, his voice is different—softer, like he's choosing his words carefully.

"You know Caroline grew up watching our parents' marriage fall apart, right? Dad checked out years before he actually left. Mom pretended everything was fine until it wasn't. And then one day, he was just... gone."

I turn to look at him. "She's never talked about that."

"She doesn't. It's not her style." Jake sighs. "But it messed her up, man. Made her think that everyone leaves eventually, so why bother getting attached? She builds walls so high, sometimes I think even she forgets there's a person underneath."

"So what are you saying?"

"I'm saying my sister is an idiot." A ghost of a smile crosses his face. "And so are you, if you let her push you away without a fight."

"She said—"

"I know what she said. I also know what I see. She looks at you like you're the only person in the world." He claps me on the shoulder. "She's scared, Ben. That's not the same as not wanting you."

"So what do I do?"

Jake leans back in with a grin that reminds me exactly why we've been friends for twenty years.

"You're a cop. Figure it out." He pauses. "But maybe don't wait too long. She's got a job offer in Boston. Trying to decide if she should take it."

With that, he turns on his heel and leaves me to my thoughts.

A job offer. In Boston.

I sit there, heart pounding, as everything clicks into place.

She's not just ending our arrangement. She's thinking about leaving. Running away from Firelight Falls, from her family, from everything she's built here.

From me.

Donna's voice echoes in my head. *If you let her walk away without at least telling her how you feel, you'll regret it for the rest of your life.*

I grab my phone.

Ben: Annie. I need your help.

Annie: Finally. I thought you'd never ask.

Annie: Tell me everything.

Seventeen

CAROLINE

THE BOSTON JOB OFFER sits in my inbox like a ticking bomb.

Senior Associate position at my old firm. Corner office, six-figure salary, the kind of career trajectory I used to dream about before I traded it all for small-town life.

I should be excited. This is everything I worked for—the validation that I didn't throw away five years of clawing my way up the ladder, that I could walk back into that world and pick up where I left off.

Instead, I stare at the email and feel nothing.

"You're moping."

I look up to find Annie standing in my kitchen doorway, arms crossed, a paper bag from the bakery in one hand.

"I'm not moping. I'm working."

"You're staring at your laptop like it personally offended you." She sets the bag on the table—muffins, from the smell of it—and drops into the chair across from me. "You've been 'working' for five days. You haven't been to the bakery. You haven't been to the nursing home to visit your mom. Jake says you're dodging his calls."

"I've been busy."

"You've been hiding." Annie's voice is gentler than I expected. "Talk to me, Caroline. What happened with Ben?"

The sound of his name brings tears to my eyes. I close my laptop, buying time.

"Nothing happened. We just... decided to end things. It wasn't working."

"Wasn't working," Annie repeats the words flatly. "The man who looked at you like you hung the moon. The woman who laughed more in the last few weeks than she has in years. That wasn't working."

"It was complicated."

"Love usually is."

"It wasn't—" I stop. Swallow. "It wasn't love, Annie. It was just... a thing. A temporary thing."

Annie is quiet for a long moment, studying me with sharp eyes that see too much.

"You know," she says finally, "when Jake came back to Firelight Falls, I was terrified. Twenty years of pretending I was over him, and then suddenly he was everywhere—at the bakery, at town events, looking at me like no time had passed at all."

"Annie—"

"I pushed him away. Told myself all the reasons it wouldn't work. We were too different, too much had happened, it was too late." She reaches across the table and takes my hand. "And then I almost lost him. For real, this time. And I realized that being scared of getting hurt is a terrible reason to give up on something that could make you happy."

My eyes are burning. I blink hard. "It's not the same."

"Isn't it?" She squeezes my hand. "Caroline, I've watched you build walls your entire life. After your dad left, after Jake left, after every person who was supposed to stay decided to go. And I get it—it's easier to leave first than to be left. But Ben isn't going anywhere. He's been here his whole life. He's not the leaving type."

"You don't know that."

"I know him. I've known him forever, it seems like." She stands, pulling a muffin from the bag and setting it in front of me. "And I know you. You're miserable, Caroline. You've been miserable since the Fourth of July. That's not what 'ending something that wasn't working' looks like. That's what heartbreak looks like."

I don't have an answer for that.

Annie kisses the top of my head on her way out. "Eat the muffin. Call your brother. And maybe think about whether being safe is really better than being happy."

The door closes behind her, and I'm alone with my cold laptop and my unanswered emails and the growing certainty that I've ruined the best thing that ever happened to me.

I visit Mom that afternoon.

It's a good day—she knows who I am, knows where she is, even remembers that Jake got married last spring. We sit in her room, sorting through old photo albums while nurses bustle down the hall.

"You look tired, sweetheart," Mom says, peering at me over her reading glasses. "Are you sleeping?"

"I'm fine, Mom."

"You're not fine. You have that look." She taps a photo of me at age twelve, gap-toothed and scowling at the camera. "The same look you had when Tommy Morrison broke up with you in seventh grade."

"I barely remember Tommy Morrison."

"You cried for a week." She turns the page, then stops at a photo I haven't seen in years—me and Jake and Dad, all of us squinting into the sun at some long-ago Rangers game. "Your father used to get that look too. When he was trying to convince himself he'd made the right choice."

My throat tightens. "Mom—"

"He thought leaving was easier than staying." She traces Dad's face with one finger. "He was wrong. Running away doesn't fix anything. It just means you're miserable somewhere else."

"I'm not running away."

She looks at me—really looks, with the sharp clarity that comes and goes like the weather these days.

"Aren't you?"

I don't have an answer.

"That nice policeman," she says suddenly. "The one with the kind eyes. Where is he? He hasn't been by in a while."

"We're not... we're not seeing each other anymore, Mom."

"Why not?"

Because I was scared. Because I pushed him away before he could leave me first. Because I'm so terrified of ending up alone that I guarantee it every time.

"It's complicated," I say instead.

Mom pats my hand, her skin papery and soft. "Love is simple, sweetheart. People make it complicated." She yawns, her energy fading the way it does these days. "I liked him. He looked at you the way your father used to look at me. Before everything went wrong."

She drifts off a few minutes later, and I sit there holding her hand, tears sliding down my cheeks.

Everyone keeps telling me the same thing. Annie, Mom, even Jake in his gruff, indirect way.

Ben looked at me like I was something special.

And I threw it away because I was too scared to believe it was real.

Eighteen

BEN

"Okay, here's what I'm thinking."

Annie spreads a napkin across the bakery counter like it's a battle map. It's after hours—she closed early so we could strategize without an audience—and the smell of day-old pastries hangs in the air.

"We stage a grand gesture. Something public, something romantic. Maybe you can ride through town on a horse with a giant bouquet of roses?"

"I'm not riding a horse."

"Fine, no horse. But we need something big. Something that shows her you're serious."

I shake my head. "That's not Caroline. She'd hate a big public spectacle. It would feel like pressure, like I'm trying to manipulate her into a response."

Annie deflates slightly. "Okay, fair point. So what does Caroline like?"

I think about it. The quiet moments—watching fireworks, eating soggy sandwiches at the duck pond, sitting in my parents' kitchen while chaos swirled around us. The way she lit up at the baseball game, not because of the crowd but because she was doing something she loved with people who cared about her.

"She likes feeling safe," I say slowly. "She likes knowing she has an escape route. She spent so long being the one who holds everything together that she doesn't know how to let someone take care of her."

"So show her she can."

"How?"

Annie taps her chin. "Where's your place? The spot that means something to both of you?"

I think about the painting class, the pizzeria, the duck pond, and the baseball stadium. All good memories, but none of them feel right for this.

And then it hits me.

"The bakery," I say. "Right here. This is where it started."

Annie's face lights up. "The morning I tried to set her up with Pastor Mike's nephew. You bought her coffee and walked her to her car."

"And asked her to fake date me like an idiot."

"An idiot who fell in love." Annie grins. "Okay. Here's what we're going to do."

We plan for an hour. Annie texts Jake for intel—apparently Caroline's been holed up at home, barely eating, refusing to talk about what happened. The Boston job is still on the table, but she hasn't responded yet.

"That's good," Annie says. "It means she's not sure. If she really wanted to leave, she would have said yes already."

"Or she's just taking her time."

"Caroline doesn't take her time. She makes decisions like she's in a courtroom—fast, certain, no looking back." Annie pokes me in the chest. "The fact that she's hesitating means something is holding her here."

"You think it's me?"

"I think you won't know unless you ask."

She's right. I hate that she's right.

"Tomorrow," I say. "I'll do it tomorrow morning. Her usual time."

"I'll make sure she comes in. Leave that part to me."

I stand to leave, but Annie catches my arm.

"Ben." Her expression is serious now, all the scheming energy gone. "She's my sister. Not by blood, but in every way that matters. If you hurt her—"

"I won't."

"You better not. Because if you do, I'll put something in your coffee that'll make you regret it."

"Noted."

She releases me with a smile. "Good luck. You're going to need it."

I don't sleep that night.

I lie in bed, staring at the ceiling, rehearsing what I'm going to say. I've never been good with words—give me a traffic stop or a chicken chase any day—but this is too important to mess up.

Caroline Colton walked into my life with her speeding tickets and her sharp tongue, and somehow, without meaning to, I fell completely in love with her.

Now I just have to convince her that love isn't something to be afraid of.

That I'm not going anywhere.

That she's worth fighting for, even when she's the one pushing me away.

When the sun comes up, I'm still awake.

I shower, shave, and put on the green shirt she once said brought out
the warmth in my eyes. I grab my keys and my courage and head to
Annie's Bakery.

Whatever happens next, at least I'll know I tried.

At least I'll know I didn't let her go without a fight.

Nineteen

CAROLINE

A TEXT COMES AT 6:15 AM.

Annie: Emergency at the bakery. Need your help. Can you come now?

I stare at my phone, still in my pajamas, hair a disaster, eyes puffy from another night of not sleeping.

Caroline: What kind of emergency?

Annie: The kind where I need you here in 20 minutes. Please, Caroline. It's important.

I sigh. I've been avoiding the bakery—avoiding everywhere Ben might be—but Annie has done so much for me. If she needs help, I can't say no.

Caroline: Fine. Be there soon.

I throw on jeans and a sweater, twist my hair into a messy bun, and don't bother with makeup. If Annie's having some kind of bakery crisis, she won't care what I look like.

The drive to Main Street is quiet, the town still waking up. I park in my usual spot and push through the bakery door, the familiar bell chiming overhead.

"Annie? What's the emer—"

I stop.

The bakery is empty. No customers, no Annie behind the counter, no smell of fresh pastries. Just soft morning light streaming through the windows and a single table set up in the middle of the room with two cups of coffee and a small vase of wildflowers.

Yellow and purple. Just like the ones Ben brought to our first date.

"Annie's not here."

I spin around. Ben is standing by the door I just walked through, and he must have been waiting outside because I didn't see him when I came in. He's wearing the green shirt I love, and his expression is somewhere between terrified and determined.

"What is this?" My voice comes out sharper than I intended. "What's going on?"

"I needed to talk to you." He takes a step closer. "And I figured you'd keep avoiding me unless someone tricked you into showing up."

"So, you and Annie ambushed me."

"Technically, Annie ambushed you. I just showed up." Another step. "Will you sit down? Please? Five minutes. That's all I'm asking."

I should leave. I should walk right past him and out the door and back to my safe, lonely house, where I can keep pretending I made the right choice.

But my feet won't move.

"Five minutes," I hear myself say.

We sit across from each other at the little table, the wildflowers between us like a peace offering. Ben slides one of the coffees toward me—black, the way I like it—and wraps his hands around his own cup like he needs something to hold onto.

"I had a speech prepared," he says. "I was up all night working on it. But now that you're here, I can't remember a single word."

"Ben—"

"So, I'm just going to say it." He looks up, and his eyes are that impossible shade of brown that's haunted me for weeks. "I'm in love with you, Caroline."

The words rush over me like a wave at the ocean. I open my mouth, but nothing comes out.

"I know that's not what you want to hear," he continues. "I know you ended things because you were scared, or because you thought it was easier, or because you convinced yourself this was never real. But it was real for me. It was real from the moment you argued with me about your speeding ticket. Maybe even before that."

"Ben, I—"

"I'm not finished." He reaches across the table and takes my hand. I should pull away, but I don't. I can't. "You told me once that you don't do anything halfway. Well, neither do I. And I can't just let you walk away—let you take that job in Boston and disappear from my life—without telling you the truth."

"How do you know about the job?"

"Jake." A ghost of a smile. "He's worried about you. Everyone's worried about you."

"I haven't decided yet."

"I know." His thumb traces circles on the back of my hand, and I feel it everywhere. "And I'm not here to tell you what to do. If you want to go back to Boston, I'll drive you to the airport myself. If you want to stay but you don't want me, I'll respect that. I'll wave at you on Main Street and pretend it doesn't kill me."

My eyes are burning. I blink hard.

"But if there's any part of you—any part at all—that feels what I feel…" He squeezes my hand. "Then stay, not for your mom, not for Jake, not for anyone else. Stay for you. Stay because Firelight Falls is your home now, whether you want to admit it or not. Stay because you deserve to be happy, Caroline. And I think—I hope—that maybe I make you happy."

A tear slides down my cheek. I swipe at it, furious with myself for crying.

"You're infuriating," I manage.

"I know."

"You pull me over for no reason. You buy my coffee without asking. You show up at my house with wildflowers and take me to painting classes and introduce me to your entire extended family—"

"All true."

"And you make me laugh." My voice cracks. "You make me laugh, Ben. No one has made me laugh like that in years."

"Is that a good thing?"

"It's terrifying." I look at him and feel the last of my protective walls crumble. "You're terrifying. Because I spent my whole life convincing myself that I don't need anyone, that it's safer to be alone, that everyone leaves eventually, so why bother getting attached. And then you showed up with your ridiculous smile and your terrible paintings and your family who treats me like I belong, and I—"

I stop. The words are stuck in my throat, too big and too scary to say out loud.

"You what?" Ben asks softly.

"I fell in love with you." The admission comes out like a confession, like something shameful. "I fell in love with you, and it scared me so much that I pushed you away before you could do it first. Because that's what I do, that's what I've always done."

"Caroline—"

"I'm sorry." The tears are falling freely now, and I don't bother wiping them away. "I'm sorry I ended things. I'm sorry I avoided you. I'm sorry I'm so broken that I can't just let myself be happy without waiting for the other shoe to drop."

Ben stands up. For a horrible second, I think he's leaving—that I've said too much, that I've scared him away the way I scare everyone away.

But he doesn't leave.

He rounds the table, pulls me to my feet, and cups my face in his hands.

"You're not broken," he says. "You're careful. You're guarded. You've been hurt, and you're trying to protect yourself. But Caroline—" His thumbs brush away my tears. "You don't have to protect yourself from me. I'm not going anywhere. I'm not your father. I'm not anyone who's ever left you. I'm just a guy who's completely, hopelessly in love with you and has been since you told me my traffic stop was a waste of taxpayer resources."

A laugh bubbles up through my tears. "It was."

"Probably." He's smiling now, that infuriating smile that used to drive me crazy and now just makes me want to kiss him. "So what do you say, Counselor? Think maybe we could try this for real? No contracts, no timelines, no exit strategies. Just you and me, figuring it out as we go."

I think about the Boston job, sitting unanswered in my inbox. I think about my mom, and Jake, and Annie, and this town that somehow became home again when I wasn't looking.

I think about the way Ben looked at me during the fireworks, like I was the only person in the world.

"I'm scared," I admit.

"I know. Me too." He leans his forehead against mine. "But I'd rather be scared with you than safe without you."

And finally, for the first time in my life, I stop running.

I close the distance between us and kiss him.

Twenty

BEN

She's kissing me.

Caroline Colton—stubborn, brilliant, infuriating Caroline—is kissing me in the middle of Annie's Bakery, and it's nothing like the kiss at the baseball game. That kiss was for show, for the cameras, for thirty thousand strangers who wanted a love story.

This kiss is just for us.

She tastes like coffee and salt from her tears, and her hands are fisted in the front of my shirt like she's afraid I'll disappear. I wrap my arms around her waist and pull her closer, and she makes a small sound against my mouth that I want to hear every day for the rest of my life.

When we finally break apart, we're both breathing hard. Her eyes are red-rimmed, her cheeks are wet, and she's the most beautiful thing I've ever seen.

"So," I say, a little dazed. "Does this mean you're staying?"

"I'm staying." She laughs—that bright, surprised laugh I fell in love with. "I'm staying, you idiot. I can't believe you made me cry before eight in the morning."

"I'll make it up to you."

"You'd better."

The bell above the door chimes, and we both turn to find Annie frozen in the doorway, a tray of muffins in her hands and an expression of barely contained glee on her face.

"Oh, don't mind me," she says, sliding behind the counter. "Just pretend I'm not here."

"You set this up," Caroline accuses, but there's no heat in it.

"I facilitated. There's a difference." Annie starts arranging muffins in the display case, deliberately not looking at us. "So? Did it work? Are you two finally done being idiots?"

I look at Caroline. She looks at me.

"Yeah," I say, reaching for her hand. "I think we are."

"Thank goodness." Annie pulls out her phone. "I'm texting Jake. And Elena. And probably the entire town, honestly. This is the best news I've had all month."

"Annie—"

"Oh, let her." Caroline squeezes my hand, and when I look at her, she's smiling. A real smile, unguarded and warm and aimed right at me. "The whole town's going to find out, anyway. Might as well let her have her moment."

"You're sure about this?" I ask quietly, searching her face. "No contracts, no safety nets. Just us."

"I'm sure." She rises on her toes and kisses me again, soft and quick and full of promise. "I'm done running, Ben. I'm done being scared. I just want to be with you."

"That," I say, pulling her into my arms, "can definitely be arranged."

Behind us, Annie is already on the phone, her voice carrying across the empty bakery.

"Elena? It's Annie. You're going to want to sit down for this. Your son finally got his act together."

Caroline buries her face in my chest, laughing.

And standing there in the morning light, surrounded by the smell of coffee and fresh muffins and the sound of Annie spreading the news to everyone who will listen, I know with absolute certainty that this is exactly where I'm supposed to be.

Not because of some arrangement or contract or fake dating scheme.

But because Caroline Colton chose me.

And I'm going to spend the rest of my life making sure she never regrets it.

Epilogue

Six Months Later

CAROLINE

The Ramirez backyard has never been louder.

Maddie, Jake's daughter, is chasing a handful of kids from the extended family through the sprinklers, shrieking with delight. Marco is stretched out in a lawn chair with Lucas asleep on his chest, looking like a man who's learned to nap through anything. My brother Jake is at the grill with Roberto, the two of them locked in a heated debate about charcoal versus propane that's been going on for twenty minutes. Annie and Elena are in the kitchen, collaborating on some kind of fusion dessert that involves both cinnamon rolls and tres leches cake, and based on the laughter echoing through the screen door, they are having a great time.

"You're staring."

I turn to find Ben beside me, two glasses of lemonade in his hands. He's wearing the green shirt I love—the one he wore the morning he told me he loved me—and his hair is messy from tossing a football with the guys.

"I'm observing," I correct, taking the lemonade. "There's a difference."

"Uh-huh." He wraps an arm around my waist and pulls me close. "What are you observing?"

"This." I gesture at the chaos in front of us—two families who've somehow become one, woven together by marriage and friendship and Sunday dinners that now happen every week. "I never thought I'd have this."

"Have what?"

"A family that feels like home."

Ben doesn't say anything. He just presses a kiss to my temple and holds me tighter.

I almost walked away from all of this. I'd convinced myself that running was easier than staying, and nearly let fear cost me everything.

I declined the job offer the same day Ben told me he loved me. Sent the email from my phone at Annie's bakery, sitting at that little table with wildflowers between us, while Ben held my hand and Annie pretended not to eavesdrop from behind the counter.

I haven't regretted it for a single second.

"Caroline!" Elena appears on the back porch, waving a wooden spoon. "Come taste this frosting. Annie says it needs more vanilla, but I think she's wrong."

"I'm not wrong!" Annie's voice floats out from inside.

"You're a little wrong!"

I laugh and disentangle myself from Ben's arms. "Duty calls."

"Go, save them from themselves." He steals a quick kiss before releasing me. "I'll be here."

· · · ●·● ● · · ·

BEN

I find Caroline by the dessert table an hour later, sneaking a second piece of the cinnamon roll tres leches monstrosity that Annie and my mother created.

"Caught you."

She doesn't even look guilty. "It's delicious. Your mother and Annie should open a fusion bakery."

"Don't say that too loud. They'll actually do it."

She laughs, and the sound still hits me right in the chest. I don't think I'll ever get tired of making Caroline laugh.

"Hey." I take her hand, pulling her away from the dessert table and toward the quieter edge of the yard, near the old fence where my father's garden grows wild. "Can I show you something?"

"Mysterious." But she follows, lacing her fingers through mine. "Should I be worried?"

"Probably."

The garden is my mother's pride and joy—tomatoes, peppers, and herbs she uses in everything she cooks. But there's a corner that's always been mine, a patch of wildflowers my grandmother planted. Yellow and purple, growing wild and stubborn, blooming even when everything else has faded.

"These are beautiful," Caroline says, kneeling down to touch the petals. "I didn't know these were here."

"My abuela planted them. Said they were the colors of joy and devotion." I crouch beside her. "I picked your first bouquet from here."

She looks up at me, something soft in her expression. "You did?"

"Yeah." I reach into my pocket, my heart hammering. "I wanted to bring you here because... it's special. You're special."

"Ben—"

"I know it's only been a few months. I know that's fast. And I'm not asking you to answer today, or tomorrow, or even this year." I pull out the small velvet box and watch her eyes go wide. "But I wanted you to know that I'm sure. I've been sure since the day you ate soggy sandwiches at the duck pond and laughed instead of yelling at me."

"Ben." Her voice is a whisper.

I open the box. The ring is simple—a single diamond, nothing flashy, because Caroline has never been about flash. It was my grandmother's, reset in a new band. Something old and something new, just like us.

"Caroline Colton," I say, "I love you. I love your sharp tongue and your guarded heart and the way you argue about zoning laws like they're a matter of life and death. I love that you stayed—not for your mom, not for Jake, but for yourself. And I want to spend the rest of my life giving you reasons to keep staying."

She's crying. I'm probably crying too—I can't tell anymore.

"So this is me, asking. Not right now, but someday. Whenever you're ready, will you marry me?"

She stares at the ring for a long moment. Then she looks up at me, tears streaming down her face, and smiles.

"Yes."

"Yes?"

"Yes, you idiot." She launches herself at me, and I catch her, laughing, the ring box pressed between us. "I don't need someday. I don't need to wait. I'm done waiting, Ben. I'm done being careful. I just want you. Forever."

I slide the ring onto her finger, silently thanking Annie for finding out her ring size, and then I kiss her. Long and slow and full of promise, the kind of kiss that says this is just the beginning.

When we break apart, she's grinning through her tears.

"Your mother is going to lose her mind."

"She's going to take full credit for this."

"She should. She basically bullied us into falling in love."

"Pretty sure we did that ourselves."

"With help." She looks down at the ring on her finger, then back at me. "I love you, Ben Ramirez. Even when you pull me over for no reason."

"I love you too, Caroline Colton." I press my forehead to hers. "Even when you're speeding."

"I was going seven over. One time."

"Three times."

"The first two don't count."

"They absolutely count."

She laughs, and I kiss her again, and somewhere behind us, I hear my mother shriek with joy—which means she's spotted us through the kitchen window and the entire party is about to descend.

But I don't care.

Because Caroline is wearing my grandmother's ring, and she said yes, and I can't wait to give her my last name.

The End

· · · ● · ● · ● · · ·

Thank you so much for reading Ben and Caroline's story. I would love it if you would leave a quick review. Even a star rating helps others know if this would be a book for them.

If you love small-town romances, couples who find their way, and swoony cinnamon roll heroes, check out my Piney Brook Wishes series.

Join my newsletter to stay up to date with all things Tia Marlee. www.tiamarlee.com/newsletter

About Tia

Tia Marlee resides in Central Texas with her husband and three teenage children. When she isn't writing, Tia enjoys reading, embroidery and spending time with her family. Tia is the author of sweet, no-steam, small-town, contemporary romance and romantic comedy. Her books are like Hallmark meets real life with a dash of humor.

Follow Tia on Facebook, Instagram, or check out her website for more information.

Let's Stay In Touch

You can find me at my website: https://tiamarlee.com
Follow me:
Facebook: https://tinyurl.com/FBTiaMarlee
Instagram: https://tinyurl.com/IGTiaMarlee
Amazon: https://tinyurl.com/AmazonTiaMarlee
BookBub: https://tinyurl.com/BBTiaMarlee
Goodreads: https://tinyurl.com/GRTiaMarlee

Join my reader group: https://tinyurl.com/TiaMarleeReaderGroup

Also By Tia Marlee

Piney Brook Wishes Series

His Christmas Wish

Sweet Summertime Wishes

Wishing for the Girl Next Door

A Soldier's Wish

Her New Year's Wish

The Piney Brook Wishes Box Set

The Coffee Loft Series

Bean Wishing for a Latte Love

You Mocha Me Crazy

A Brewtiful Kind of Love

Coffee Loft Collection

Apple Blossom Ranch Series

His to Adore

His to Have

His to Hold
His to Love
His to Cherish
Hers to Treasure

Sugar and Sirens
Still Yours, Always Mine
Catch Me, If You Can
Sweeter With You
A Little Bit Married
The Last First Kiss

A Little Bit of Christmas
Merry & Bright: The Great Light Fight
Gnome Sweet Home
The Candy Cane Parade
Mistletoe at Midnight